BAREFOOT HUSAIN

Anjali Raghbeer

illustrated by **Soumya Menon**

Tulika

Jai stared at the paintings, lost in a swirl of colour. Around him,
the rest of his class wandered about the Museum of Modern Art.

His teacher went on about artists and imagination. Soon her voice faded
away into a soft drone. "Jai, are you coming?" he heard someone say.

"One minute," Jai replied as he peered at the canvases, fascinated by the shapes and colours. When he looked up, he found himself alone. The room had many doors. Which way did they go?

"Hey, where's everyone?" he shouted.

A man with a white beard appeared in the doorway. Jai caught his breath. The man peered at Jai through thick black-rimmed glasses. His bony hands stroked his beard. Jai pushed the hair out of his eyes for a better look. He stared and he stared. He'd seen that face in a book at home about famous artists.

"M. F. Husain!" said Jai.

The man looked at him.

"Yes," he sighed.

"Are you lost too?" asked Jai, wondering why Husain looked so sad.

"No, no. It's just that my show opens today in the other room. But... but I can't be there," said Husain.

"Why not?" asked Jai.

"I've lost my shoes," said Husain.

"So?"

Husain waved his paint-stained hands in the air. "I promised Zubeida, my sister, I'd wear them, and now I can't find them."

"But you never wear shoes," said Jai.
He remembered it from somewhere.

"I know, but a promise is a promise," Husain replied.

"I'll help you find them," Jai blurted out in a rush of excitement.

Husain raised his eyebrows and began to doodle. What seemed like a few bold lines at first, turned into a majestic horse! The horse stepped out of the sketchbook, tossed its mane and whinnied.

"It's real!" cried Jai.

He stared at the striking beast, astonished.

A tiny smile turned the corners of
Husain's mouth.

"Let's go find the shoes!" he said.

The next thing Jai knew, he was galloping down the street on a grey stallion. His heart hammered even as he held on tight.

Just as suddenly the horse stopped at a busy Mumbai crossing. Cars and buses blasted their horns. A huge canvas hoarding stood at the corner. A man sat on top of a tall ladder. In one hand he held a picture of a film star, while with the other he put finishing touches to a larger than life version of him onto the canvas.

"This is what I did when I was fifteen," said Husain, appearing beside him.

"Painted film posters?" gulped Jai.

Husain nodded.

"Shabab bhai! Have you seen my shoes?" yelled Husain.

But his voice was drowned by the noisy traffic.

"Jai, you'll have to go up and ask."

Jai scurried up the ladder. He felt dizzy as he reached the top.

Husain looked tinier than an ant. Everything looked tiny.

Only the movie star looked enormous.

"Shabab bhai, have you seen Husain saab's shoes?" asked Jai.

"Does it look like I have? Will I keep them in my pocket up here?" yelled Shabab.

"Sorry," said Jai.

Shabab wagged his brush at him. Blue blotches speckled Jai's shirt.

"Try Khichdiwala's dhaba. Husain's there every day for lunch."

Painting of a film hoarding

Jai scrambled down.

"Let's go to Khichdiwala's dhaba," he said.

Husain doodled again. He drew a narrow street bustling with people. The sweet smell of freshly cooked halwa pulled Jai to Khichdiwala's dhaba.

This detail from 'Zameen' shows familiar traditional symbols of an Indian village, like pots and a woman churning butter. But it is painted in a modern style and with oil paints, a Western medium.

"Husain saab has sent me," said Jai. "Have you seen his shoes?"

"No, son," said Khichdiwala. "But give him these laddoos. They're his favourite."

Jai's mouth watered.

"Try Souza saab's house," said Khichdiwala, handing Jai the laddoos.

Jai stopped at the doorway to stare at the picture of a woman.

"Husain painted my mother in return for free meals," said Khichdiwala.

"I knew he would be famous one day."

Jai could have sworn that the lady in the picture winked at him.

From a series on umbrellas

Husain sat on the pavement nibbling roasted corn.

Jai opened the box of laddoos.

"Tasty, no?" asked Husain.

Jai nodded as he gulped some down.

It began to pour.

Husain painted umbrellas – black, grey, blue, red and pink.

Jai and Husain floated away with the umbrellas.

They landed in front of a white house with a wooden staircase.

Jai ran all the way up to Souza's studio.

He was Husain's artist friend.

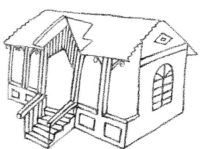

An old man opened the door. "Husain saab sent me," said Jai. "He..."

"Alright, alright, sit here please," said Souza.

Souza began to draw. Sometimes he stopped to look at Jai. Jai heard the scritch-scritch of his pen.

After what seemed to be a long time he said, "Perfect!"

Jai leaned over to see — and shrank back in surprise. Souza had drawn a child with three heads.

"Abstract art, see that? You don't have to paint things the way they look," said Souza.

Not knowing what to say, Jai nodded.

"What was it you wanted?" asked Souza vaguely.

"Never mind," said Jai.

From a series called 'Homage to C. V. Raman', in honour of the famous scientist who symbolised vigyan or science for Husain

Jai dragged his feet. Husain would be so disappointed. But to his surprise,

Husain was dancing — in the rain!

"I know where I must have left my shoes," he shouted.

"Where?" asked Jai, smiling again.

Husain sketched a Fiat with Krishna's dancing gopis and horses drawn on it.

"Jump in," he said.

A painting based on Husain's film 'Gaja Gamini', starring well-known actress Madhuri Dixit. 'Gaja gamini' means 'one who walks (gracefully) like an elephant'.

They rushed. They honked. They waded their way to Mehboob Studios in Filmistan. Husain pulled Jai inside.

"Madhuri, Madhuri, you must know where my shoes are?" he said.

"Huzoor, I've never seen you wear shoes!" the actress laughed.

"How about your movie set?" asked Jai, pointing to a board that said 'Gaja Gamini'.

"Brilliant boy!" Husain turned around.

Jai searched high and low.

A director walked in. "Is he the new child actor?" he asked, looking at Jai.

Jai grabbed Husain's hand and ran back to the car.

Also from the 'Gaja Gamini' series, which was a tribute to all women from everywhere, down the ages

It poured and it poured and it poured.

Husain said, "We've been to Shabab, we've been to Khichdiwala, we've been to Souza, and we've been to Madhuri."

He stared blankly at the rain.

Then he said, "Let's try this."

Husain doodled a pair of shoes.

"Hey, an Englishman's wearing them," cried Jai.

"My favourite shoes come from London," agreed Husain.

Knock! Knock! Knock! Jai saw the Englishman outside the window, in the rain.

"Young man, I need to catch up with my hunting expedition," he said.

"Will you give us your shoes if we help you?" Jai asked quickly.

"My shoes?" It poured even harder. "Well, alright," the man said.

From a series on the British Raj

The road gave way to a dense, marshy forest.
In the distance, horses neighed and elephants
trumpeted.
"I'll get off here," said the Englishman, handing
Jai the shoes.
Husain wore the shoes, wet but just right.
His face lit up.

"Now let's get you back," said Husain.

He sat down to doodle again. Nothing. He fumbled with the pencil in his bony hands.

The page remained blank. He couldn't draw. Husain looked at Jai. His hands trembled.

"I don't know what's happened," he said.

Jai felt sick to the stomach. Husain not able to draw? What was wrong?

Jai thought and thought. Husain had only just sketched shoes, then–
That's when it hit him!
"Can you draw only when you're barefoot?" he asked softly.

A silence followed, of the loudest kind.

Sketches of Ganesha, a Ramlila scene and Hanuman. Husain was deeply inspired by mythology and has done many paintings based on the 'Mahabharata' and 'Ramayana', apart from others on gods and goddesses. He calls one of his Hanuman paintings, 'The Original Superman'!

"There's only one way to check," said Jai.
Husain kicked off the shoes. He felt free!
Happily, he picked up his pencil and sketched
Jai at the museum with his class.
Jai hugged Husain.

"But what about the promise to your sister?"
he asked.
"I'll give her these laddoos. She won't
mind then," Husain laughed.

"Jai!" said his teacher. "Where have you been?"
But Jai was watching Husain walk away to his show.
Barefoot.

Looking at M. F. Husain's paintings

Maqbool Fida Husain has never followed rules. He can wear a designer suit but still go barefoot. Free-spirited, he refuses to paint only in a studio, like most artists – he paints anywhere. When Husain was a little boy, his family moved from the small village of Pandharpur where he was born in 1915, to Indore. He would go off on his bicycle to paint the landscape around the city, or write poetry.

Hoo

He also learnt calligraphy, the art of writing beautifully. Through this he learnt many things about the use of lines. The painting on the left shows calligraphic writing.

When he was around 18, he went to Mumbai to earn a living. He started by painting cinema hoardings, perched high up or in the middle of traffic. Once he had to paint a 40-foot high cutout of an actress overnight. Right after the last tram went by at midnight, Husain laid the huge canvas across the road and began to paint. He finished just before the first tram came by early next morning! Work like this trained him for something he is especially known for now – painting confidently and quickly over large areas. In the photograph on the right, you can see him painting a wall mural with a long brush, standing high up there quite comfortably.

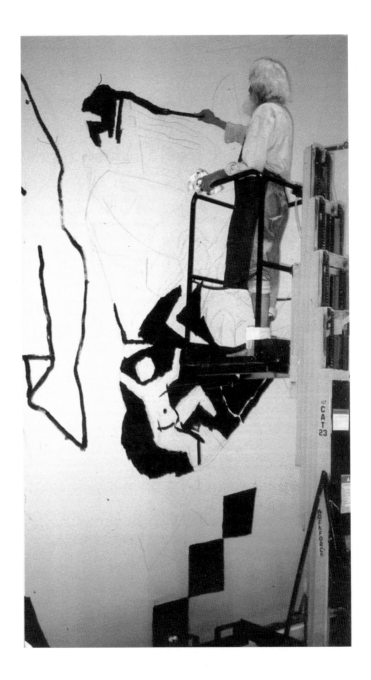

In this way, he taught himself art. As he developed as an artist he was influenced by other art styles – the work of European painters, Indian miniatures, Mathura sculptures, and tribal and folk art. Husain's paintings have historical scenes, everyday scenes, film stars, gods, musical instruments … or just umbrellas!

Shatranj Ke Khilari, 1990s

Kumbhar, 1947

Gaja Gamini, 2000

Raagmala, 1980s

Ganesha

Untitled, 1960s

Horses, 2000s

Bangalore Races, 2000

But he is most famous for his dramatic horses. They have been inspired mainly by Duldul (the horse that belonged to Prophet Mohammad's grandson), the powerful white horse of the Ashwamedha yagyas, and the horses painted by Chinese artist Ch'i Pai-Shih. He describes his horses as "charging like a dragon in the front and graceful and elegant from the back".

A painting specially done for the book Kerala: God's Own Country, *2000*

When we look at Husain's art, what is most striking is his brilliant use of colour. And in his paintings – unlike in Western styles of art – colour is also a symbol, it has meaning. Husain has always been fascinated by the way symbols are so much a part of daily life in India. For example, an orange spot on a stone is immediately understood as Hanuman, even if it has no eyes or nose or tail.

With over 20,000 paintings, Husain still has the same enthusiastic spirit. After some groups in India created trouble over a few of his paintings, he had to go and live in London and Dubai. But nothing stops him from painting. As he says, "They can put me in a jungle. Still, I can create."

To Mom, whose zest for life and aesthetic sense have always inspired me – AR

The Looking at Art series:

A Tree in my Village – Paritosh Sen, painter

My Name is Amrita – Amrita Sher-Gil, painter

A Trail of Paint – Jamini Roy, painter

The Veena Player – Ravi Varma, painter

Barefoot Husain – M. F. Husain, painter

Stitching Stories – Gujarati folk embroidery

The Little Clay Horse – Sonabai Rajawar, terracotta sculptor (forthcoming)

Barefoot Husain (English)

ISBN 978-81-8146-652-5
© story Anjali Raghbeer
© illustrations Tulika Publishers
First published in India, 2009
Reprinted in 2011

Designed by Radhika Menon

Our deepest thanks to M. F. Husain for going through the book and offering valuable comments, and for giving permission to reproduce pictures of his paintings for this particular publication only. M. F. Husain holds the copyright to his paintings and they may not be used in part or whole in any manner without the written permission of the artist for the same.

Thanks also to Najma Husain for her warm and active cooperation.

Published by
Tulika Publishers, 13 Prithvi Avenue, Abhiramapuram, Chennai 600 018, India
email tulikabooks@vsnl.com website www.tulikabooks.com

Printed and bound by
Sudarsan Graphics, 27 Neelkanta Mehta Street, T. Nagar, Chennai 600 017, India

To order books visit www.tulikabooks.com